Jakers!™

What's Hatching?

adapted by Catherine Lukas   images by Entara Ltd.

SIMON SPOTLIGHT
New York London Toronto Sydney

Hello, there. I'm Grandpa Piggley. Gather round and I'll tell you a story about when I was growing up down on Raloo Farm. *Jakers!* What fun we used to have . . .

Based on the TV series *Jakers! The Adventures of Piggley Winks* created by Entara Ltd.

SIMON SPOTLIGHT
An imprint of Simon & Schuster Children's Publishing Division
1230 Avenue of the Americas, New York, New York 10020
Manufactured in the United States of America
First Edition
2 4 6 8 10 9 7 5 3 1
ISBN-13: 978-0-689-87861-9
ISBN-10: 0-689-87861-3

It was a beautiful spring day. Piggley, Ferny, and Dannan were on an important mission. They were hunting for dragons!

"Let's look in the old castle ruins!" suggested Dannan.

"Good idea," said Piggley. "We brave knights are sure to find a big, scary dragon with fiery breath and a spiny back!"

The dragon hunters marched through the archway of the old stone castle.

Piggley leaped onto a rock, waving his wooden-spoon sword.

Suddenly his sword slipped out of his hand and sailed over the old stone wall.

"Oh, no," called Piggley. "My sword!"

The three explorers hurried after it.

Piggley spied his sword in the grass next to something large, round, and white.

"Jakers!" he shouted. "Look at the size of that egg!"

Ferny and Dannan came to see. All three stared down at the strange egg.

"Janey Mack! Do you think the Easter Bunny dropped it here?" asked Ferny.

"No," Dannan replied. "It's not a chocolate egg."

"It's too big to have a baby bird inside," said Piggley. "There is only one thing it *can* be."

"A *dragon's* egg!" said all three at the same time.

"If that's a baby dragon," said Ferny, "then where's the mother dragon?"

Dannan pointed to the opening of a spooky-looking cave nearby. "She must be in there," she whispered. "Someone had better return this egg to her before she gets mad."

Dannan and Ferny both looked at Piggley, who gulped.

"Fine," he said. "I'll take it."

Dannan and Ferny watched Piggley creep into the dark cave. He was gone for a few minutes. Then . . .

"Jakers!" yelled Piggley, tearing out of the cave, still clutching the egg. "I can't see the mother in there, but I heard lots of spooky noises. Let's go!" He dashed away as fast as he could.

"Well, if we can't find the mother dragon, then we'll just have to care for this baby dragon ourselves," said Dannan.

"Maybe we could find a mother who is willing to keep it warm while it's waiting to hatch," said Piggley.

"Great idea!" said Ferny. "Let's find a mom!"

"Why not try the experts?" said Dannan, pointing toward the henhouse.

But the chickens didn't want anything to do with the enormous egg. "Janey Mack!" cried Ferny, who barely managed to catch the precious egg after a hen had tossed it out of her nest. "Maybe we should find someone else to sit on our egg!"

They crept into the sheep pen and slipped the egg under the warm wool of a sleeping sheep named Wiley. Then Ferny, Piggley, and Dannan hurried out of the barn.

When Wiley woke up, he noticed a big lump underneath him.

"Hopping hair balls! I've laid an egg!" said Wiley. "Hey, everybody! I'm a mother!" he yelled to the other sheep.

But the egg seemed to have a mind of its own. It rolled away from Wiley.
It rolled and rolled and rolled . . . all the way out of the barn and stopped at
Piggley's feet.

"He followed us!" wailed Ferny.

"He thinks we're his mother!" said Dannan. "We'll just have to sit on the egg ourselves. We'll take turns. Who wants to be first?"

Piggley and Ferny looked at Dannan. She sighed.

They made a cozy nest with warm blankets, and then Dannan settled herself carefully atop the egg. Piggley and Ferny left Dannan some water in case she got thirsty, then went off to look for food for the little dragon to eat after it had hatched.

Dannan sat and sat and sat. After what seemed like a very long time, she slid off her perch. "I must go to the bathroom, little egg!" she said. "I'll be right back!"

No sooner had Dannan hurried out than the egg began to crack!

Not long after that, Ferny and Piggley returned.
"What's happened to the dragon egg?" asked Ferny.
"It's hatched!" said Piggley. "And look! There's the little dragon!"

Just then Dannan rushed back to the barn, along with Molly. All four of them tried to catch the little creature. Molly finally managed to trap it under a bucket. "Let's bring it into the kitchen!" she said excitedly.

"What are you up to?" asked Piggley and Molly's mother as they rushed inside.

"We've found a baby dragon!" explained Piggley.

"A dragon, eh?" she said, and peered into the bucket. The little creature honked at her and hopped out of the bucket onto the floor.

"What's all the commotion in here?" asked Mr. Winks.

"Piggley's found himself a little dragon," said Mrs. Winks with a twinkle in her eye. "Have a look!"

Mr. Winks looked under the table. "Why, that's no dragon!" he said.

"What is it then?" asked all of the kids at the same time.

"It's a cygnet!" Mr. Winks explained. "A cygnet is a baby swan."

"A swan?" said Piggley.

"He's a wild animal, Piggley," said Piggley's father. "He belongs outdoors with his mother."

"We tried to find her!" said Piggley.

"Have another look tomorrow," said his father. "She's bound to be down at the pond somewhere. Meanwhile, tonight, *you're* going to look after him!"

"I can do that, Dad!" Piggley said eagerly.

The next morning they brought the baby swan to the pond, where they found its mother anxiously looking around for her baby.

"I'm going to miss you, dragon," Piggley said to the baby swan. "But now it's time for you to go back to the wild where you belong."

The little bird seemed to understand and hurried off to join its family.